The Little Red Hen

REWRITTEN BY ELIZABETH LANE

ILLUSTRATED BY GUY FRANCIS

The little red hen was always tidy and busy. One day as she was sweeping her yard, she found something.

"A grain of wheat!" she said. "Just what I need to make some bread!"

"Who will help me plant this wheat?" she asked her barnyard friends.

"Not I," said the cat.
"Not I," said the duck.
"Not I," said the pig.

"Then I'll do it myself," said the little red hen. And so she did.

The little red hen watered and hoed. The wheat grew tall. "Who will help me harvest this wheat?" asked the little red hen.

"Not I," said the cat.
"Not I," said the duck.
"Not I," said the pig.

"Then I'll do it myself," said the little red hen. And so she did.

"It's time to grind this wheat into flour," said the little red hen. "Who will help me carry the wheat to the mill?"

"Not I," said the cat.
"Not I," said the duck.
"Not I," said the pig.

"Then I'll do it myself," said the little red hen. And so she did.

At last the flour was ready. “Who will help me mix the bread?” asked the little red hen.

"Not I," said the cat.
"Not I," said the duck.
"Not I," said the pig.

"Then I'll do it myself," said the little red hen. And so she did.

The bread dough rose into nice, plump loaves. “Who will help me bake the bread?” asked the little red hen.

"Not I," said the cat.
"Not I," said the duck.
"Not I," said the pig.

“Then I’ll do it myself,” said the little red hen. And so she did.

When the bread was done, it smelled wonderful. “Now, who will help me eat this yummy bread?” asked the little red hen.

“I will!” said the cat.
“I will!” said the duck.
“I will!” said the pig.

"No, you won't,"
said the little red hen.
"I did all the work.
My chicks and I shall
eat all the bread."

She cut big, thick slices and spread them with butter and jam. Then she called her baby chicks.

They pecked up
the nice, hot bread to
the very last crumb.